가출

〈K-픽션〉 시리즈는 한국문학의 젊은 상상력입니다. 최근 발표된 가장 우수하고 흥미로운 작품을 엄선하여 출간하는 〈K-픽션〉은 한국문학의 생생한 현장을 국내외 독자들과 실시간으로 공유하고자 기획되었습니다. 〈바이링궐 에디션 한국 대표 소설〉 시리즈를 통해 검증된 탁월한 번역진이 참여하여 원작의 재미와 품격을 최대한 살린 〈K-픽션〉 시리즈는 매 계절마다 새로운 작품을 선보입니다.

The 〈K-Fiction〉 Series represents the brightest of young imaginative voices in contemporary Korean fiction. This series consists of a wide range of outstanding contemporary Korean short stories that the editorial board of *ASIA* carefully selects each season. These stories are then translated by professional Korean literature translators, all of whom take special care to faithfully convey the pieces' original tones and grace. We hope that, each and every season, these exceptional young Korean voices will delight and challenge all of you, our treasured readers both here and abroad.

K-Fiction Series

가출
Run Away

조남주 | 전미세리 옮김
Written by Cho Nam-joo
Translated by Jeon Miseli

ASIA
PUBLISHERS

차례
Contents

가출
Run Away

아버지가 가출했다. 엄마의 전화를 받은 것은 퇴근길 지하철에서였다. 나는 순간 가출을 출가로 착각했다.

"응? 아버지 절에도 안 다니잖아."

– 가출하셨다고. 가, 출. 집 나갔단 말이다.

차라리 출가했다고 하면 믿었을 것이다. 올해 나이 일흔둘. 치매 등 정신 질환은 없다. 일곱 살이나 어린 아내에게 꼬박꼬박 존댓말을 쓰는 아버지. 그렇지만 엄마가 숟가락과 젓가락과 마실 물까지 완벽하게 제자리에 놓아야 식탁에 와 앉는 아버지. 정년까지 근무하는 동안 양가 부모님 장례 이외에는 한 번도 결근한 적이 없는, 삼남매가 태어나던 날도 출근했다는 아버지. 눈에 보이

"Father's run away from home." I was on the subway train on my way home from work when I got a phone call from Mother. At the moment, I mistook the word *ga'chul* for *chulga* and thought Father had joined the Buddhist priesthood.

"What? Father's not even a Buddhist."

"I said *ga'chul*. *ga—chul*. He's gone, left home for good."

I would have believed her if she had said Father had become a Buddhist priest. Father is seventy-two years old and has no mental illnesses like dementia. He always uses the polite speech with Mother who is seven years younger than him. And yet, he will never come to sit at the dining table until Mother finishes setting the table perfectly with

지 않는 것은 믿지 않는다며 신용카드도 만들지 않고 자동이체도 하지 않고 인터넷 뱅킹도 하지 않는 아버지. 그런 아버지가 가출을 했단다.

뭐? 뭐라고? 라고 열 번쯤 되묻다가 다음 역에서 일단 내렸다. 하필 사람들이 몰리는 환승역이었다. 환승 통로를 향해 질주하는 무리 사이에 끼어 한참을 떠밀려가다 겨우 빠져나왔을 때 전화는 이미 끊겨 있었다. 나는 자판기에서 차가운 캔 커피를 뽑아 들고 플랫폼 구석의 빈 의자에 앉아 다시 전화를 걸었다.

"무슨 소리야? 아버지가 왜 가출을 해? 언제?"

– 실은 한 달이 다 돼간다.

"뭐? 근데 왜 이제까지 말을 안 했어?"

– 금방 들어올 줄 알았지. 자식들한테도 남세스럽다. 이 나이에 이게 무슨 망신이니?

"가출 확실해? 납치나 실종 뭐 그런 거 아니고?"

– 편지 써놓고 나갔어.

중학교 때 나도 편지를 써놓고 가출을 시도한 적이 있다. 친구네서 몰래 술을 마시다 걸려서 엄마에게 죽도록 맞은 다음 날이었다. 내가 잘못을 하긴 했지만 그래도 이런 비인간적인 대우는 참을 수 없으니 이제 나

spoons, chopsticks, and glasses of water all in place. He never missed a day of work until he retired, except for the funeral days of his and Mother's parents. He went to work even on the day each of his three children was born. Insisting that he does not trust anything he cannot see with his own eyes, he refuses to get credit cards, wire-transfer money, or use the Internet-banking. Now, that father of mine, according to Mother, had walked out on his family.

"What? What's that again?" I repeated the same question about ten more times before I got off the train at the next station. It happened to be one of the transfer stations always crowded with people. I was swept away for a while in the throngs of people who were running along the transfer passages; by the time I managed to make my way out of the crowd, the phone had already been disconnected. I got a can of cold coffee from the vending machine and sat down on an empty bench in a corner of the platform. And I called my mother again.

"What d'you mean? What on earth made him leave home? When was it?"

"To tell the truth, it's been almost a month now."

"What? Why then haven't you said anything to us?"

"I thought he'd return soon enough. It's so embarrassing to tell even you children. What a shame! At my age!"

"Are you sure Father's left of his own free will? Couldn't it be a case of abduction or missing person?"

를 찾지 말라는 취지의 편지를 장황하게 썼던 것 같다. 일단 학교를 마치고 친구네 집에서 놀았다. 하지만 저녁 먹을 시간이 되자 친구 언니가 눈치를 줘서 나올 수밖에 없었다. 딱히 갈 데가 없었다. 동네 놀이터에서 시간을 보내다가 집에 갔는데 마침 아무도 없기에 그냥 가출하지 않기로 했다. 그런데 책상에 두고 나갔던 편지가 없었다. 어쩔 수 없이 가방을 메고 구두를 들고 내 방 옷장 속에 들어가 숨었다. 그대로 깜빡 잠이 들었는데 엄마가 저녁 먹으라며 방문을 두드리는 소리가 들렸다. 잠결에 옷장에서 나와 구두를 든 채로 마루에 나가 밥상 앞에 앉았다.

"구두 현관에 놓고 와라. 가방도 내려놓고."

엄마는 태연히 말했고 나도 순순히 구두와 가방을 내려놓고 밥을 먹었다. 오빠들도 아무 말 하지 않았다. 밥을 다 먹고 평소처럼 옷을 갈아입고 텔레비전을 보다가 잤다. 아버지도 혹시 옷장 안에 있는 게 아닐까. 낡은 구두를 들고 옷장 속에 웅크리고 앉은 아버지를 생각했다. 한 달씩이나. 다리가 많이 저릴 텐데.

─ 여보세요? 듣고 있어? 경찰에 신고할까?

"가출도 신고를 받아주나? 내가 한번 알아볼게. 오빠

12

"He left a note for us."

As a junior-high student, I tried to run away from home too, leaving a letter behind. It was the day after I got severely beaten by my mother, having been caught drinking secretly at my friend's. I wrote a long letter to the effect that though admitting my mistake, I refused to take such an inhumane treatment and they should not to try to find me. After school that day, I went to my friend's and played with her. But when it was time for dinner, my friend's elder sister looked displeased with me staying on and I had no choice but to leave. Having no other place to go, I spent some time at the neighborhood playground and then went back home. There was no one at home, so I just decided not to run away. But the problem was, the letter I had left on my desk was gone. I decided to hide inside the closet in my room, with the book bag on my back and shoes in my hand. I fell asleep there and was woken up by my mother knocking on the door, asking me to come out and eat dinner. Half asleep and still holding the shoes in my hand, I came out of the closet, walked towards the dining table, and sat down to eat.

"Go put your shoes in the entrance hall. And put your book bag down, too."

Mother said as if nothing had happened; and I meekly put away the shoes and the book bag, and ate dinner. My elder brothers did not say anything,

들은 알고?"

―그게…… 애기 좀 해주라. 차마 입이 안 떨어진다.

입이 안 떨어지기는 나도 마찬가지다. 아, 아버지, 차라리 출가를 하시지. 속세의 모든 고통과 번뇌를 내려놓고 종교에 귀의했다면 아버지를 잠시 원망하고 오래 안쓰러워하고 말았을 텐데. 심호흡을 한번 한 후 오빠들에게 차례로 전화를 했다. 큰오빠는 한참 대답이 없다가 알았다며 지금 집으로 가겠다고 했다. 작은오빠는 그게 무슨 말도 안 되는 소리냐고 길길 날뛰더니 오늘은 결혼기념일이니 내일 모이자고 했다. 오빠야말로 말도 안 되는 소리 말고 당장 집으로 오라고 말했다.

휴대폰을 꺼내 지하철 노선도를 확인했다. 집에 가려면 지하철을 두 번이나 갈아타야 한다. 아버지는 왜 가출을 해가지고. 본가에 도착하면 아홉 시, 두 시간 정도 엄마에게 설명을 듣고 대책회의를 한다 치면 열한 시, 다시 내 집에 도착하면 열두 시 반, 씻고 어쩌고 하면 한시 반. 아, 아버지는 왜 가출을 해가지고!

골목 입구에서부터 청국장 냄새가 진동을 했다. 어느 집에서 이렇게 늦게 저녁밥을 먹나 했는데 우리 집이었

either. After dinner, I changed clothes, watched TV and went to bed as usual. 'Isn't father also hiding himself in the closet?' I imagined my father crouching down in the closet with his worn-out shoes in his hand. For as long as a month! 'Oh, he must have terrible pins and needles in his legs.'

"Hello? Are you still there? Should I call the police?"

"Can we report a runaway? Do the police take that kind of report, too? Let me find out. Do my brothers know about it?"

"Well . . . Could you please talk to them for me? I can't possibly break the news to your brothers."

'It's difficult for me, too. Ah, Father, it would have been better for you to become a Buddhist priest, renouncing all the worldly pains and desires and turning to religion. Then, we would have resented you briefly, but felt sorry for you for a long time to come.' I took a deep breath and called one brother after the other. The eldest brother was speechless for a long while and finally said he would come home right away. The second elder brother threw a fit at first, saying it did not make any sense at all; he then proposed a family meeting on the following day since that day was their wedding anniversary. I told him to quit the nonsense and come home immediately.

I checked the subway routes on my cell phone. I needed to transfer twice to go to my parents'. 'Why

다. 엄마는 그 와중에 잡채를 하고 고등어를 굽고 호박전까지 부쳤다. 큰오빠 내외와 작은오빠는 이미 밥을 먹고 있었고, 엄마는 식탁에 내 수저를 놓았다.

"왜 이렇게 늦었어? 얼른 손 씻고 와서 밥부터 먹어."

지금 밥이 넘어 가느냐고 물으려는데 작은오빠가 엄마에게 밥그릇을 내밀며 한 그릇 더 달라고 했다. 나도 별 수 없이 식탁 앞에 앉았다. 머리로는 정말 밥 먹을 기분이 아니라고 생각했지만 혀 아래로 침이 돌았다.

우리 삼남매는 어려서부터 청국장을 좋아했다. 엄마는 총각김치를 송송 썰어 아삭하게 씹히도록 하고 간 돼지고기와 으깬 두부를 넣어 아주 걸쭉하게 청국장찌개를 끓인다. 마지막으로 큰 이모가 담가주는 집된장을 한 숟갈 푹 퍼 넣으면 짭짤하고 구수한 맛이 살아나는데 아버지는 그 맛있는 청국장찌개를 너무 싫어했다. 쿰쿰한 냄새가 섬유 한 올 한 올, 머리카락 사이사이에 스며들어 도무지 빠지지 않는다는 것이다. 아버지가 야근하시는 날이 청국장찌개를 먹는 날이었는데 아버지가 정년퇴직을 하신 후 한 번도 엄마의 청국장을 먹지 못했다.

찌개를 숟갈 가득 퍼서 밥에 슥슥 비볐다. 매끄럽고

on earth did he have to run away! It'll be around nine when I arrive there, and it'll take about two hours to listen to Mother's explanation and talk about what to do. I'll be back home around half past twelve. Washing up and so on, it'll be half past one. Ah, why in the world did he have to run away!'

The alley, even from its mouth, smelled strongly of *chong'gukjang*. I wondered who among the neighbors was having dinner that late, but it turned out to be my mother, even at a time like that, making *chong'gukjang*, in addition to other dishes like *japche*, grilled mackerel and pumpkin pancake. The eldest brother, his wife, and the second elder brother were already eating and Mother put an extra set of spoon and chopsticks on the table for me.

"What kept you so long? Go wash your hands, we'll eat first."

I was about to ask how they could eat at a time like that, but then the second elder brother held out his rice bowl to Mother and asked for seconds. I could not help but sit at the table. Although my head said I was in no mood for food, my mouth was already watering.

The three of us siblings have always loved *chong'gukjang* since childhood. Mother chops young-radish *kimchi* into bite-size crisp pieces and mixes them with ground pork and crushed tofu to make a very thick pot of *chong'gukjang*. When it

뜨거운 밥알은 씹을 새도 없이 목구멍으로 홀랑홀랑 넘어갔고 배 속이 뜨끈해지며 머리에서 땀이 났다. 청국장 맛이야 말할 것도 없고 잡채는 이미 다 식었는데도 당면이 불어 끊어지지 않고 혀에 착착 감겼다. 분명 나도 같은 김치를 가져다 먹고 있는데 이상하게 본가에서 먹는 김치가 더 맛있다. 그렇게 정신없이 밥을 다 먹고 나니 이미 열 시가 넘었다.

밥을 먹을 때는 명절을 맞아 모인 것처럼 화기애애했는데 거실에 둘러앉으니 침울해졌다. 올케언니가 이리저리 눈치를 살피다가 커피를 타오겠다며 주방 쪽으로 가자 작은오빠가 낮은 목소리로 큰오빠를 나무랐다.

"형은 무슨 좋은 일이라고 형수를 여기까지 데려와?"

"우리 가족 일인데 형수도 알아야지. 넌 그럼 제수씨한테 얘기도 안 하고 왔냐?"

"당연하지. 오늘 결혼기념일이라 오랜만에 둘이 외식 좀 하려고 준이 처가에 보내놨는데. 준이 엄마 지금 혼자 술 마시고 있으니까 얼른 얘기 끝내. 나 빨리 가야 돼."

"그런 놈이 밥을 두 그릇이나 먹냐?"

오빠들을 진정시키고 엄마에게 자초지종을 물었다. 엄마는 길게 한숨부터 내쉬었다.

comes to a boil, she then adds a generous spoon-
ful of homemade soybean paste given by her elder
sister in order to bring out the savoriness. But Father hates that delicious food. He complains that
the moldy odor gets into the fibers of clothes and
even into the strands of hair, and wouldn't come
out. So, we used to eat Mother's *chong'gukjang* only
when Father was on night duty. Unfortunately, after
Father retired from work, we have never had a
chance to eat Mother's *chong'gukjang*.

I put two spoonfuls of *chong'gukjang* in my bowl
of rice and mixed it in. The soft and hot grains of
rice slid down my throat even before I could chew
them well. My stomach felt warm and my scalp began to sweat. In addition to the scrumptious
chong'gukjang, the *japche* noodles, no longer warm
but still not gone sodden at all, seemed to caress
my tongue. In fact, at my own home, I eat the same
kimchi brought from my parents', but for some reason, it always tastes better when eating at my parents'. By the time we finished devouring the food,
it was already past ten.

We were in such a happy atmosphere during the
dinner as if we had gathered there on a festive day,
but when we sat down to talk in the living room, all
of us looked heavy-hearted. After studying each
person's face, the sister-in-law got up and walked
towards the kitchen, saying that she would go
make some coffee for us. As soon as she was out

"지난달 십칠 일에, 그러니까 나 계모임 있던 날. 나갔다 왔더니 냉장고에 쪽지가 붙어있더라고."

엄마는 엉덩이를 붙인 채 뭉그적뭉그적 텔레비전장으로 기어가 서랍을 열고 쪽지를 꺼내왔다.

'내가 살면 얼마나 더 살겠니. 이제라도 내 인생 살고 싶다. 나를 찾지 마라. 저축은행 160만원은 가져간다. 미안하다.'

큰오빠가 뺏듯이 쪽지를 낚아챘다. 작은오빠가 머리를 들이밀며 소리 내 읽더니 허탈하게 웃었다.

"아버지 노망난 거 아니야?"

그때 올케가 커피 다섯 잔을 큰 쟁반에 담아 들고 왔다. 작은오빠는 입을 닫았고 큰오빠는 쪽지를 엄마에게 건넸다. 엄마는 다시 한 번 쪽지를 보더니 갑자기 눈물을 뚝뚝 떨어뜨렸다.

"오늘은 오겠지, 내일은 오겠지…… 나 혼자 마음 졸이고 있다가 아무래도 이대로는 안 되겠어서. 어쩔까?"

작은오빠가 커피를 한 번 호로록 마시고는 대답했다.

"어쩌긴 뭘 어째? 경찰에 신고해야지."

"실종도 아니고 가출인데 경찰에서 열심히 찾아주겠냐? 쪽지 봐라. 이건 명백히 자의에 의한 가출이야. 그

of earshot, the second elder brother, under his breath, criticized the eldest brother:

"What d'you mean by bringing your wife here at a time like this?"

"It concerns all of us in the family. Of course, she should know what's going on. You mean you haven't told your wife about it yet?"

"Of course not. Today's our wedding anniversary, so the two of us had a plan to eat out for the first time in a long while. She's even sent Jun'ee to her parents'. Now she's drinking alone, so I've got to go home soon. Let's finish our discussion as quickly as possible."

"And yet you've eaten two bowls of rice!"

I told my brothers to calm down and asked Mother to tell us what exactly had happened. Mother uttered a long sigh first:

"On the 17th of last month, I had a *gye* club meeting. When I returned home, I found a note on the fridge door."

Mother, instead of getting up, pushed herself sluggishly towards the TV cabinet, dragging her behind along the surface of the floor. She then took out a piece of paper from a drawer and came back with it in her hand.

The eldest brother snatched the note from Mother's hand. The second elder brother leaned over and read the note loudly:

'I no longer have a long time left to live. Too late

렇다고 아버지가 어디 몸이 불편한 것도 아니고 사리분별을 못하는 것도 아니고. 멀쩡한 성인 남자가 가출을 했는데 경찰은 무슨 경찰이야? 차라리 흥신소 알아보는 게 빠르겠다."

"형은 왜 그렇게 부정적으로 생각해? 아버지 나이를 생각해봐. 진짜 갑자기 노망나서 나간 걸 수도 있다고. 우리가 모르는 돈 문제나 원한 문제가 있을 수도 있고 어쩌면 범죄에 연루된 걸 수도 있어."

"부정적인 건 내가 아니라 너야 인마. 자꾸 재수 없는 소리 할래?"

오빠들의 말싸움을 끊으려고 내가 다시 엄마에게 물었다.

"어디 연락해 볼 데 없어?"

"늬 아버지가 연락하는 사람이 있니. 퇴직한 후로는 매일 집에서 텔레비전만 보던 양반인데. 큰집에는 안부 전화하는 척 하면서 한번 전화해 봤는데 전혀 모르는 눈치고. 휴대폰에 너희들 전화번호랑 큰집 번호, 고모 번호밖에 없더라."

"휴대폰 놓고 나갔어?"

"아무것도 안 가지고 갔어. 팬티 한 장 안 들고 나갔다

as it is, I'd like to spend the rest of my life the way I really want to. Don't look for me. I'm taking 1.6 million won from the savings account. I'm sorry.'

After reading the note, the second elder brother gave a hollow laugh and said:

"Father must have gone senile, don't you think?"

At the moment, the sister-in-law came back carrying a big tray with five cups of coffee on it. The second elder brother fell silent and the eldest brother handed the note back to Mother. Upon reading it once more, Mother burst into tears.

"I've been telling myself, 'He'll come home today or tomorrow' . . . But now I know, worrying all by myself isn't going to solve the problem. What can we do?"

Taking a sip of coffee noisily, the second elder brother answered:

"There's nothing we can do but report it to the police."

"Father's not a missing person. He left home of his own accord. Would the police take it seriously? Loot at the note. He made it clear that he was leaving home voluntarily. Moreover, he's neither physically disabled nor mentally impaired. A sane and healthy adult man has left home. Reporting to the police? Nonsense! A better thing to do is hire a private detective."

"Brother, aren't you being too negative? You know how old Father is. He may have suddenly

니까. 왜 이번 가을에 산 등산복 있잖아. 등산도 안 하면서 무슨 바람이 불어서 등산복인지 모르겠다고 내가 그랬잖아. 그 등산복 입고 운동화 신고 막내가 사준 녹음기만 들고 나갔어. 보니까 백육십 만원은 전날 찾았더라고."

작은오빠가 내게 물었다.

"아버지한테 녹음기 사드렸어?"

"녹음기 아니고 엠피쓰리. 요즘 젊은 사람들 다 귀에 뭐 꽂고 다니는데 뭐 듣는 거냐고 하시더라고. 스마트폰으로 음악도 듣고 라디오도 듣고 그런다고 폰 바꿔드리겠다 그러니까 됐대. 그래서 음악만 들을 수 있는 작은 기계도 있다고 하니까 싼 걸로 하나 사 달라대. 트로트 음악 백 곡 정도 넣어 드렸지."

"언제?"

"한참 됐어. 서너 달?"

"그동안 너한테 따로 연락 온 것도 없고?"

"응. 오빠한테는 있었어?"

"아니. 아버지가 너한테는 유난하시잖아."

큰오빠도 고개를 끄덕였다.

"그러게. 늦둥이 막내딸이라고 따로 데리고 다니면서

gone senile, or had some money problems that we're not aware of, or fallen a victim to somebody's grudge. Or, he could have been involved in a crime for all I know."

"Look who's really negative, dude! Go ahead, keep on croaking!"

To stop their wrangling, I asked:

"Mother, don't you know anybody you can call?"

"As you know, your father keeps no contact with anyone. After retirement, he's been staying home everyday, watching TV. I already called his eldest brother's, pretending to just say hello. But they seemed to know absolutely nothing about him. The only phone numbers stored in his cell phone are yours, his eldest brother's and sister's."

"You mean he's left his cell phone behind?"

"He didn't take anything at all. Not even a pair of underpants. Remember the mountain-climbing clothes he bought this fall? I told you, I don't understand why he needs them when he never climbs mountains. Well, he walked out in those clothes and sneakers, taking with him only the recorder the youngest had bought him. It turned out that he had taken out 1.6 million won from the account the day before he left home."

The second elder brother asked me:

"Did you buy him a recorder?"

"It's not a recorder, it's an MP3 player. He once asked me what all the young people these days are

떡볶이도 사주시고 원피스도 사주시고 하여튼 엄청 예뻐하셨지. 막내 독립한다고 했을 때 난리 났던 거 생각난다. 진짜 너 머리 깎이는 줄 알았어. 근데 그런 분이 왜…… 우리 막내 시집은 어떻게 가라고."

새로 옮긴 직장이 멀다는 핑계로 이 년 전 독립을 선언했을 때, 아버지는 세상 무서운 줄도 복잡한 줄도 모르고 철없는 소리 한다고 펄쩍펄쩍 뛰셨다.

"결혼하기 전까지는 아버지가 네 보호자다. 내가 우리 딸 지금처럼 티 없이 지켜줄 거야."

"저도 곧 스물아홉이고 사회생활이 오 년 차인데 제가 정말 티끌 하나 없을 것 같으세요?"

아버지는 내가 티끌 정도가 아니라 움푹움푹 옹이투성이이며 스스로 그 옹이들을 별로 대단치 않게 생각한다는 것을 알고는 크게 충격을 받았다. 내 가치관과 태도를 문제 삼는 아버지와 매일매일 부딪혔고 감정의 골이 계속 깊어져 도저히 함께 살 수 없는 지경이 되어버렸다.

결국 아버지가 손을 들었다. 내 결혼 자금에 보태려고 모아두었다는 삼천만 원 통장을 집 구할 때 쓰라며 내밀었다. 대신 이 년 후, 그러니까 독립해 살 집의 임대계

listening to through something inserted in their ears. So, I told him they use smart phones to listen to music or radio broadcasting. I offered to get him a new cell phone, but he refused. When I told him there is a small device with which one can only listen to music, he asked me to buy a cheap one for him. So, I bought one and downloaded about a hundred foxtrot songs before I gave it to him."

"When was that?"

"It's been a while. Three or four months?"

"Has he ever called you since then?"

"No. What about you, brother, has he called you?"

"No. But he's always making a fuss of you, isn't he?"

The eldest brother nodded in agreement:

"That's true. He adored you, the youngest daughter he had late in his life. He used to take you around, buying things for you like *tteokbokki* and dresses. I still remember how upset he was when you decided to move out to live on your own. I really thought you would get your hair cropped. But now, why on earth such a loving father . . . Even before he marries off his youngest child. Shouldn't he be worried?"

On the excuse that my new workplace was too far away from home, I declared independence two years ago. Father was absolutely livid about the idea, saying that I was talking nonsense because I

약 만기가 되면 결혼하라는 조건을 달았다. 어차피 남자친구와 이 년 더 돈 벌어서 결혼하자고 얘기가 끝난 상태였고 보증금이 커지면 더 좋은 집을 구할 수 있으니 나한테는 전혀 나쁠 것 없는 제안이라 냉큼 수락했다.

종종 외롭기도 하고 아무리 일인 가구라도 혼자 살림 다 하고 밥 챙겨 먹으며 회사 다니려니 힘들긴 했지만 부모님과 함께 사는 것보다는 좋았다. 독립해 살면서 아버지와의 관계도 빠르게 회복되었다. 그렇게 시간이 후딱 지나 봄이면 약속했던 이 년이 된다.

다행인지 불행인지 나는 남자친구를 계속 잘 만났고 아버지는 겨울에 상견례하고 봄에 시집보내면 딱 좋겠다고 하셨다. 그런데 이제 아버지가 없다. 정말 시집은 어떻게 가라고. 남자친구한테는 뭐라고 말하지. 상견례와 결혼식 때 엄마 혼자 나가야 하나. 사실 아버지가 집을 나간 마당에 결혼을 한다는 것도 웃기는 일이다. 결혼을 안 한다면 부동산 계약을 연장해야 하나. 그런 생각들이 꼬리에 꼬리를 물고 이어지다가 집 나간 아버지 걱정보다 나 살 걱정 먼저 하고 있는 스스로가 한심해졌다.

고개를 빠르게 흔들어 잡생각들을 털어낸 후 선언하

didn't know how dangerous and complicated the outside world was.

"Before you get married, I'm still your guardian. And it's my job to keep my daughter as pure and spotless as she is now."

"Father, I'm almost twenty-nine and have had a social life for five years. Do you really believe I'm pure and spotless now?"

Learning that I was full of deep knotholes, let alone spots, and that I thought nothing of the knotholes myself, Father was profoundly shocked. From that day on, I was constantly at war with my father who found my sense of values and attitude problematic, until it became impossible for us to live in the same house because of the unbridgeable emotional gap between us.

In the end, Father surrendered. He then handed me a bankbook with a deposit balance of 30,000,000 won, which he said he had been saving for my wedding, and asked me to use it to rent a place for myself. It was on condition that two years later, that is, by the end of the rental contract, I would get married. The thing is, my boyfriend and I had already agreed to get married two years later when we have saved enough money. Moreover, I could get a better place for myself with more security money. Since I had nothing to lose, I agreed to the condition right away.

While living alone, I often felt lonely and found it

듯 내가 전단지를 만들어 붙이겠다고 말했다. 큰오빠는 경찰에 신고하겠단다. 잘하는 짓인지는 모르겠지만 엄마가 큰아버지와 고모에게도 알리겠다고 했다. 큰오빠가 작은오빠에게 물었다.

"넌 뭐 할 거야?"

"이렇게 해도 안 되면 그때 내가 사람 붙여서 찾는 거 한번 알아볼게."

"어떻게 된 게 넌 집안일에 항상 뒷짐이야? 나랑 막내한테만 아버지냐? 너한테도 아버지야. 평생 입히고 먹이고 가르쳐 주셨다고!"

"말은 똑바로 하자. 평생 형이 입던 것만 입고 눈칫밥 먹고 나만 대학 못 나왔어."

"네가 공부 안 해서 대학 못 간 걸 왜 아버지 탓을 해?"

"막내는 자기가 공부해서 간 거지만 형은 아니잖아. 삼수해서 겨우 삼류대학 간 주제에. 나도 형처럼 삼수시켜주고 학원비 대줬으면 형보다 좋은 대학 갈 수 있었어."

오빠들의 목소리가 점점 커지자 엄마가 소리를 꽥 질렀다.

"환갑 돼서도 싸울래? 내 제사상 앞에서도 싸울래? 나

difficult to go to work everyday and do all the cooking and housekeeping by myself. Nevertheless, it was better than living with my parents. My relationship with Father was also being mended fast. Time quickly passed and come spring, it would be the end of the promised period of two years. Fortunately or unfortunately, my boyfriend and I got along very well, and Father said it would be perfect if we could have the *sang'gyonrye* (the first formal meeting before a wedding between the families of the bride and the groom) that winter and the wedding the coming spring. 'But Father is no longer with us. What indeed am I supposed to do? What do I tell my boyfriend? Is Mother going to come to the *sang'gyonrye* and wedding alone without Father? In fact, it seems ridiculous for me to get married not long after my father ran away from home. If I decide not to get married, should I extend the rental contract?' As a series of thoughts like these went through my mind one after another, I realized that I was concerned more about my own wellbeing than about my father's, and I felt ashamed of myself.

I shook my head hard to chase off those thoughts and said resolutely, as if I were making a declaration, that I would make fliers and paste them up around the neighborhood. The eldest brother said he would report it to the police. Mother said she would let Uncle and Aunt know, although I wasn't sure if it was the right thing to do.

너희 엄마고 여기서 제일 어른이야. 어떻게 부모 앞에서 이렇게 예의 없는 행동을 해? 아무도 내 의견 먼저 묻지 않더라. 나 혼자 지내는 거 걱정하지도 않고. 헛 키웠다, 헛 키웠어. 며느리 보기 부끄럽다!"

놀랐다. 엄마의 목소리가 커서도 아니고 화를 내서도 아니었다. 발음이 너무 좋았다. 식탁에 둘러 앉아, 과일을 앞에 두고, 차를 마시며 종종 가족들이 이야기를 나눌 때면 항상 아버지가 의견을 내고 엄마는 혼잣말하듯 중얼거리고 오빠들과 나는 고개를 끄덕였다. 가족의 이사, 누군가의 진학이나 취업 같은 중요한 결정도, 여행지, 외식 메뉴, 텔레비전 채널 같은 사소한 결정도 결국은 아버지 뜻대로 되었고 엄마는 늘 중얼거리는 사람이었다. 엄마도 저렇게 간결한 문장과 정확한 발음으로 의견을 말 할 수 있구나, 신기했다.

소득 없이 일차 회의를 마쳤다. 가파른 골목에 빠듯하게 세워진 오빠들의 차가 무사히 나가는 것을 봐주고 나도 정류장으로 가려는데 엄마가 눈을 찡긋거리며 팔을 잡아끌었다. 혹시나 오빠들에게는 말 못한 중요 정보라도 있는 걸까. 나는 순순히 엄마를 따라 다시 집으로 들어갔고 엄마는 전자레인지 위에서 종이 뭉치를 꺼

The eldest brother asked the second elder brother:

"What're you gonna do?"

"If all of your ideas fail, then I'll find a way to hire a professional."

"What's the matter with you? You're always keeping aloof from our family affairs. Is he father to only me and the youngest? He is your father, too, you know. He's fed you and clothed all your life!"

"Oh c'mon! Let's get the facts straight here. All my life, I've worn your old clothes, never felt welcomed at home, and I'm the only one who's not a university graduate.

"You failed to get admission because you didn't study hard. How's that Father's fault?"

"I admit the youngest studied hard and got the admission. But your case is different. You failed twice, and only on the third try, you barely gained the admission, to a third-rate university at that. If I had been allowed to make three attempts and given money to take lessons at private institutes like you had been, I would have got in a better university than yours."

As the brothers' voices were getting louder, Mother suddenly screamed:

"Until when are you gonna fight like this? Even after your sixtieth birthdays? Even during the memorial service for me? I'm your mother and oldest among us. How can you be so rude in your mother's presence? We've been talking about your fa-

내 내밀었다. 전기요금, 상하수도요금, 도시가스요금, 휴대전화요금…… 각종 공과금의 지로용지들이었다.

"이거 그냥 은행 들고 가면 되는 거야?"

엄마가 왜 한 달이 다 되어가는 이 시점에 아버지의 가출 사실을 털어놓았는지 알 것 같았다. 공과금 납부 마감일이 다가오고 있었던 것이다. 엄마는 그동안 아버지께 딱 살림에 필요한 금액만 생활비로 받아쓰셨을 뿐 돈이 얼마나 어디로 나가는지, 또 어디로 모이는지 전혀 알지 못하고 살았다. 아버지는 퇴직한 후 은행을 여유 있게 다닐 수 있어 좋다고 말했다. 공과금 내는 날이면 점심도 제대로 못 먹었다는 것이다. 공공기관이나 은행 업무는 출근하지 않는 엄마에게 맡기지 그랬느냐고 하자 아버지는 아니라고 했다.

"그건 내 일이지. 그러라고 내가 이 집에 있는 건데."

아버지의 일. 아버지가 자신의 일이라고 한 일이 또 뭐가 있더라. 두 번이나 대입에 실패한 큰오빠가 이제 자신은 대학을 포기하고 취직해 동생들 학비를 벌겠다고 했을 때도 아버지는 같은 말을 했다. 회사가 어려워 몇 달째 월급이 나오지 않고 있다는 사실을 뒤늦게 알게 된 엄마에게도 그랬다. 할머니가 쓰러지셨다는 연락

ther here, haven't we? Then how come no one's asked my opinion first? What's worse, none of you seems to worry about me being left all alone here. You thankless kids! I tried to raise you properly, but in vain! I'm ashamed even to think how foolish I look to my daughter-in-law!"

I was surprised. Not because Mother's voice was loud, nor because she was angry. But because she enunciated each word so clearly. Whenever we made conversation, sitting around the dining table, sharing a dish of fruit, or drinking tea, it was always Father who came up with ideas, while Mother just murmured something as if to herself, and my brothers and I responded simply by nodding our heads. Not only the important decisions made when someone in the family moved, entered school or took a job, but also such trivial decisions as choosing travel destinations, restaurants or TV channels were all made by Father; and Mother was always the mumbler. That is why I was so amazed to hear Mother articulate herself, making such concise sentences and clear pronunciations.

Our first meeting was fruitless. After I helped my brothers pull away their cars that had been parked tightly along the narrow, steep alley, I was about to walk to the bus station when Mother winked at me, pulling me by the hand. 'Is there something she wants to tell me? Perhaps some information she's reluctant to share with my brothers?' I obediently

을 받고 병원 갈 준비를 하는 우리 삼남매를 만류하면서도 말했다. 그건 내 일이다.

이제 이 집에는 평생 아버지가 자신의 일이라고 생각하며 도맡아 온 크고 작은 일들을 처리할 사람이 없다. 엄마에게 대신 내주겠다고 하려다가 엄마도 할 줄 알아야겠다 싶어서 방법을 설명했다. 번호표를 뽑고 기다렸다가 창구로 가서 직원의 도움을 받는다. 엄마는 내 간단한 설명을 듣고는 입을 삐죽거렸다.

"그 말은 나도 하겠다."

예상대로 경찰은 단순가출로 처리하고 적극적으로 수사하지 않았다. 아버지 사진이 담긴 전단지는 두 시간 만에 엄마가 모두 떼어버렸다. 쓸데없이 장난전화만 많이 와서라고 했지만 동네에 소문나는 것이 싫었던 것 같다. 아버지에게서는 연락이 없고 날씨만 더 추워졌다.

토요일에 두 번째 가족회의를 위해 모였다. 엄마는 이번에도 청국장을 끓이고 갈비를 굽고 도토리묵을 무쳤다. 들깨향이 진하게 풍기는 도토리묵 무침은 내가 제일 좋아하는 반찬이고 이번에는 내가 두 그릇을 먹었다. 큰오빠는 갈비를 너무 열심히 뜯어서 번들거리는

followed Mother back into the house and Mother took out a bundle of paper from the cupboard above the microwave oven and held it out to me. The electricity bill, water bill, natural gas bill, cell phone bill . . . They were various giro bills for the public utility.

"All I have to do is just take these bills to the bank and pay, right?"

I realized why Mother had chosen that particular time, that is, almost a month after Father left home, to tell us about his disappearance. The bills were due pretty soon. Mother had always been given by Father the exact amount of money necessary for housekeeping, but she had no idea how much was spent for what or how much was saved where. After retirement, Father said it was nice to have free time to go to the bank. When he was still working, I was told, he had difficulty finding time to have lunch on the days the bills were due. When I said he should have let Mother take care of the visits to banks or public offices, Father said no:

"That's my job. That's why I'm here in this family."

Come to think of it, there were other occasions when Father referred to "my job," that is, "Father's job." When the eldest brother, having failed to pass the university admission for the second time, said he would give up the university education and work to earn money for his younger brother and sister's school expenses, Father said the same

입술로 엄마를 향해 이제 밥 차리지 말라고 말하고는 꺼어어어어억, 길게 트림을 했다.

올케언니들은 모두 일이 있어 오지 못했고, 엄마와 삼남매가 거실에 앉아 한숨만 쉬고 있는 사이 제 아빠들을 따라온 조카 셋이 아버지 방을 차지했다. 뛰지 말란 소리를 숨 쉬듯 듣는 아파트 키드 조카들에게 단독주택인 할아버지 할머니 집은 세상 제일 신나는 놀이터인 듯했다. 조카들은 책상에서 뛰어 내리고, 바퀴 달린 의자를 타고, 온갖 서랍을 다 열어 안에 있는 내용물들을 몽땅 끄집어냈다. 막판에는 거울 옆에 걸려 있는 얇은 일력을 한 장 한 장 뜯어내어 구겨서 뭉친 후 눈싸움하듯 던지고 놀다가 까르르까르르 웃으며 거실까지 튀어나왔다. 엄마가 급히 커피잔을 손으로 가리며 소리쳤다.

"커피 쏟아져, 이 녀석들아. 방에 들어가서 놀아!"

오늘따라 왜 이렇게들 요란하게 노나 생각하고 있는데 조카들의 목소리가 들렸다. 이 방에서 오랜만에 노니까 되게 재밌다! 신기한 것도 많아졌어!

내가 독립했을 때 아버지는 내 방을 자신의 서재로 꾸몄다. 사실 아버지는 책도 별로 없고 책 읽는 것도 좋아하지 않는데 굳이 책상을 두고 가라고 하셨다. 왼쪽

thing. When Mother found out belatedly that Father had not been paid by his company for several months because of some financial problems, he said the same thing. When we children, hearing that Grandmother had collapsed, were getting ready to go to the hospital, he stopped us and said, "That's my job."

Now, there was no one in this household who could assume those heavy or light responsibilities that Father had shouldered alone, thinking that they were his job, and no one else's. I was going to say to Mother that I would pay the bills for her, but then I changed my mind, thinking that Mother should learn to do it herself, and began to explain how to do it:

"First, you take the number ticket and wait. When it's your turn, you go to the wicket and get help from the clerk."

After listening to my brief explanation, Mother said, pouting:

"Even I can say that much."

As expected, the police treated our report as a simple case of runaway and did not investigate it in earnest. The fliers with Father's picture on them were all taken down by my mother only two hours after they were posted up. She said they were producing no useful information but prank calls, but I believe she was worried they might set rumors

에 오단 책장이 붙은 h자 모양의 책상. 내가 중학교 때부터 쓰던 것이다. 들어갈 오피스텔에 최소한의 가구들은 붙박이로 설치되어 있어 선심 쓰듯 두고 나왔다. 나중에 와서 보니 아버지는 삼국지, 논어, 기업 총수의 자서전 같은 것들로 책장을 채우고 있었다.

독립 전까지 조카들이 오는 날은 내 방 책장의 모든 책이 쏟아져 나오고 화장품 중 최소 하나는 깨지고 서랍이 뒤집어지는 날이었다. 그런데 내 방이 아버지 방이 된 후로 가족들은 열심히 조카들을 단속했다. 특별히 아버지가 방을 어지럽히지 말라고 한 것도 아니고 그 방에 귀중품이 있는 것도 아닌데 그랬다. 아버지도 괜찮으니 전처럼 놀게 두라고 하지 않았다. 시간이 지나자 아이들도 자연스럽게 작은 방은 이제 할아버지 방이고 들어가 놀면 안 되는 곳이라고 생각하는 듯했다.

이미 올해 마지막 날까지 다 뜯겨 묶음고리만 대롱대롱 매달린 일력, 계단 모양으로 책상 위에 쌓인 삼국지들, 볼이 발갛게 되어 신나게 뛰어노는 조카들. 나는 한참 아버지 방에서 시선을 떼지 못했다. 아버지가 없는 아버지 방이 낯설었고 보기 좋았고 이런 생각을 하고 있다는 사실에 죄책감이 들었다.

afloat in the neighborhood. While the weather was getting colder everyday, there was still no news from Father.

On Saturday, we had another family meeting. Mother again made *chong'gukjang*, roasted ribs and seasoned acorn jelly. Mother's acorn jelly dish with rich perilla flavor is my favorite and this time, I was the one who had two bowls of rice. The eldest brother, his lips greasy from having gorged on the roasted ribs, told Mother not to prepare meals for us anymore, before he let out a long, loud belch.

Both of the sisters-in-law had other engagements that day, so they did not come. While Mother and the three of us could do nothing but sit and sigh in the living room, my three nephews who had come with their dads were playing in Father's study. To the nephews, so-called "apartment kids" who are used to being told, almost as often as they breathe, not to jump or run at home, their grandparents' detached house was the best playground in the world. They jumped off the desk, rode the caster-wheeled chairs, opened all the drawers, and took out whatever was inside them. In the end, they tore out pages from the daily pad calendar hung on the wall beside the mirror, crumpled up each page into a ball and threw the balls at one another as if they were having a snow fight. The kids then ran out of the study into the living room, screaming with laughter. Mother quickly covered

결국 큰오빠가 홍신소 얘기를 꺼냈지만 작은오빠가 반대했다.

"안 그래도 내가 알아봤어. 근데 진행비 필요하다면서 계속 돈만 요구하고 일처리도 못하는 사람들이 엄청 많대. 그렇게 돈만 뜯겨도 그 사람들 무서워 싫은 소리도 못한다더라고."

엄마도 같은 생각이었다.

"그래. 나도 좀 찝찝하다. 그런 무서운 사람들하고 관련되는 것도 싫고 말이야."

"그럼 언제까지 이렇게 손 놓고 있을 거예요? 아버지가 어디서 뭘 하시는지, 막말로 살아 계시기는 한 건지도 모르고 있잖아. 친한 친구가 있으신 것도 아니고 휴대폰을 가지고 나가신 것도 아니고 신용카드를 쓰시는 것도 아니고. 실마리가 없어. 어디서부터 어떻게 찾아 들어가야 할지 모르겠어."

잘 쓰시지는 않지만 아버지에게는 신용카드가 있다. 내가 작년에 드린 것이다. 현금을 갖고 다니는 것이 불편하지는 않지만 어쩌다 가끔, 갑자기 친구들을 만나거나 안경을 급하게 다시 맞춰야 하거나 병원에 들를 일이 생겼을 때 신용카드가 아쉬우셨던 모양이다. 요즘은

the coffee cups with her hands and yelled:

"You'll spill the coffee, little rascals. Go back to the room and play there!"

'They're unusually loud today,' I was thinking, then I heard one of them saying: "Wow, it's so much fun to play in this room after a long time! And this room now has even more interesting things than before!"

When I moved out, Father remodeled my room into his study. As a matter of fact, he did not have many books, nor did he like reading books; and yet he asked me to leave my old desk behind. It was an h-shaped desk with a five-shelf bookcase attached to its left side. I had used it since junior high school. The studio apartment I was moving into had some basic built-in furniture, so I left the desk as if I were doing Father a kindness. Later when I visited my parents', I found the shelves filled with books like *Romance of the Three Kingdoms, the Analects of Confucius*, autobiographies written by business leaders, and the like.

Before I moved out, whenever the nephews came for a visit, all the books on the shelves in my room would be pulled down to the floor, at least one of my makeup containers would get shattered, and all the drawers would be pulled out and turned upside down. When the room became Father's study, however, the adults in the family kept the kids under strict control. They did so not because Father asked them to keep the room undisturbed, nor be-

신용카드 만드는 것도 실적이라고 들었다며 이왕이면 남자친구를 통해서 만들겠다고 하셨는데, 하필 그때 남자친구와 한 달 넘도록 냉전 중이었다. 일단 내 카드를 쓰시라고 드렸다. 남자친구 할당량을 채우려고 만들었는데 연회비만 내고 있을 뿐 거의 쓰지 않은 카드였다.

"다 큰 딸이 주는 용돈이라고 생각하세요. 너무 마음껏 쓰진 마시구요. 설마 딸을 신용불량자 만들진 않으실 거죠?"

일부러 가볍게 말했다. 아버지가 됐다 하시면 나도 농담이었던 듯 웃으며 다시 카드를 지갑에 넣으려고 했다. 아버지의 퇴직 소식을 듣고 오빠들과 내가 돈을 모아 매달 일정금액을 드리겠다고 했는데, 아버지는 자식에게 손 벌리는 부모가 어디 있느냐며 노발대발 했었다. 아버지가 생각하는 부모와 자식의 역할이 그렇다면 굳이 아버지의 마음을 불편하게 하고 싶지 않았다. 오빠들과 나는 드리지도 못할 용돈을 통장에 차곡차곡 모으기만 했다.

아버지는 내가 내민 카드를 물끄러미 바라보았다. 핑크색 바탕에 빨간 하이힐이 그려져 있는 2030 레이디 카드. 아버지는 순순히 카드를 받아 지갑에 넣으며 엄

cause some valuables were kept in it. But then, Father never told them either that it was okay to let the kids play in the room as they used to. As time passed, the children seemed to naturally accept that the small room now belonged to Grandfather, so they were not supposed to play in it anymore.

Only the binding part of the daily pad calendar, now completely stripped of its pages, was dangling from the wall. The volumes of *Romance of the Three Kingdoms* were stacked on the desk one on top of another in the shape of stairs. The nephews were having a wonderful time in the room, romping around with rosy cheeks. I could not take my eyes off Father's room for a long time. Father's room with Father gone was unfamiliar, yet looked good, I thought; and I felt guilty about it.

In the end, it was the eldest brother who brought up once more the subject of contacting a detective agency, but the second elder brother was opposed to it:

"As a matter of fact, I've already looked into it. And I heard that so many of them are not competent, and yet keep demanding money for their operating expenses. Even while being fleeced by their agencies, the clients cannot complain because they're too scared of them."

Mother also thought so:

"Yeah, I feel uneasy about it, too. I don't want to have anything to do with scary people like them."

마에게는 말하지 마라, 했다. 나는 당황해서 아무 농담도 못하고 고개만 끄덕였다. 정말 만약을 위해 갖고만 다니시는지 거의 사용하시지 않았다. 식당에서 만 삼천 원 한 번, 삼만 사천 원 한 번. 정형외과에서 이만 삼천 원. 옷가게에서 사만 천 원. 일 년이 넘는 동안 아버지가 사용한 카드 내역의 전부이고 가출 이후로는 카드를 쓰시지 않았다.

엄마와 오빠들에게 말하려다 말았다. 아버지와의 약속을 깨뜨리면서 쓰지도 않는 카드에 대해 가족들에게 떠벌리고 싶지 않았다.

두 번째 가족회의를 마친 다음 날, 그러니까 일요일 아침 아홉 시에 문자메시지가 왔다.

'web 발신 카드승인 4,500원 일시불 12/11 09:11 삼거리식당 누적 4,500원'

잠결에 메시지를 확인하고 처음에는 광고문자인 줄 알았다. 짜증을 내며 휴대폰을 던져놓고 돌아눕다가 퍼뜩 정신이 들었다. 아버지다! 아버지의 카드 사용내역이 내 휴대폰으로 안내된 것이다. 피가 순식간에 머리로 쏠려 눈이 욱신욱신했다. 큰오빠에게 전화를 걸기

"Until when, then, are we gonna sit here, doing nothing? We don't know where Father is or what he's doing. Sorry to put it bluntly, but we don't even know whether Father is still alive. It's not that he has close friends, or carries a cell phone with him. He never uses credit cards, either. We've got absolutely no clue. I don't know where to begin looking for him."

Truth to tell, Father has a credit card, though he seldom uses it. I gave it to him last year. He said that he had no problem carrying cash with him, but at times, he wished to have a credit card, for example, when he ran across a friend, or urgently needed to get a new pair of glasses, or had to pay for an unexpected hospital bill. Father heard from somewhere that these days keeping good credit-card sales records would help to get high performance ratings and wanted to get one offered by my boyfriend. But it so happened that at the time, my boyfriend and I had not spoken to each other for over a month. So, I said Father could use my card for the time being. I had got that card to help my boyfriend fill his sales quota, but I hardly used it even though I was paying the annual membership fee.

"Please, think of it as your pocket money given by your all-grown-up daughter. But don't overuse it. You don't want me to suffer a bad credit standing, do you?"

I said jokingly, on purpose. If Father said "Don't

위해 주소록을 찾다가 급히 취소했다. 침착해야 한다. 아버지는 카드를 쓸 때마다 내 휴대폰으로 문자메시지가 온다는 사실을 알고 있다. 정형외과 결제 문자가 왔을 때 어디 다치셨냐고 전화를 드렸더랬다.

"요즘은 결제하면 휴대폰으로 문자가 다 와요. 근데 그게 내 카드라 저한테 오는 거죠."

"그럼 그동안 계속 문자 받았던 거야? 이거 딸 눈치 보여서 카드도 마음대로 못 긁겠네."

아버지는 허허 웃으시고는 며칠 만에 또 카드를 사용하셨다. 이번에도 분실이나 범죄가 아니라 아버지라는 확신이 강하게 들었다. 나에게 문자메시지가 오는 것을 알면서도 삼거리식당에서 사천오백 원짜리 아침밥을 사먹고 카드로 결제한 아버지. 왜 그러셨을까.

노트북을 켜고 삼거리식당을 검색했다. 칼국수를 팔고 돼지갈비를 팔고 갈치조림을 팔고 닭백숙을 파는 삼거리식당들이 전국에 즐비했다. 카드사 홈페이지에 로그인을 하려는데 아무래도 비밀번호가 기억나지 않았다. 두 번, 세 번, 네 번을 틀렸고 주민번호를 함께 입력하라는 안내가 나왔고 그래도 두 번을 더 틀렸고 더 이상 틀리면 계정이 잠긴다는 안내가 나왔다. 고객센터로

bother," I would put the card right back in my wallet, laughing as if the whole thing was just a joke, I reckoned. When we heard the news of Father's retirement, my brothers and I said we would chip in and give Father a certain amount of money every month. But Father became livid saying, "What kind of parents would ask their children for money?" If that was what Father thought of the roles of parents and children, we did not want to unnecessarily make Father feel uncomfortable. All my brothers and I could do was regularly deposit in a bank account Father's pocket money that he himself would not accept from us.

Father stared at the card I held out. It was one of the 2030 Lady Cards, with the picture of a red high-heeled shoe against the pink background. Father quite readily took the card and put it in his wallet and said, "Don't tell your mom." Taken aback, I just nodded my head, unable to say anything, not even in joke. Nevertheless, he seemed to carry it with him only for emergencies because he rarely used it. A total of 13,000 won at a restaurant, 34,000 won at another restaurant, 23,000 won at an orthopedics clinic, 41,000 won at a men's wear store—these made up the entire list of card payments made by my father over the period of more than a year; after he left home, he no longer used the card.

I was going to tell my mother and brothers about the card, but soon changed my mind. I did not

전화를 했더니 일요일이라 분실이나 도난신고만 가능했다.

카드 도난신고를 해버릴까. 그러면 어떻게든 아버지를 찾을 수 있을 것이다. 하지만 그렇게 범인 잡듯이 아버지를 찾고 나면 아버지와 내 사이는 어떻게 될까. 우리 가족은 어떻게 될까. 경찰에 카드 결제 정보를 전할까 하는 생각도 했다. 그럼 경찰에서 빠르게 카드 결제 상점의 위치를 확인해 출동해줄까. 경찰에 그런 권한이나 능력이 있을까. 믿음이 가지 않았다.

일단 메모지를 꺼내 그동안 내가 써왔던 비밀번호들을 다 적고 입력해 본 비밀번호 여섯 개를 지웠다. 최근에 새로 만든 번호들도 지웠다. 너무 단순한 것들도 지웠다. 그렇게 주욱 지워가니 남은 번호는 두 개였고 고민 끝에 그중 하나를 입력했다. 비밀번호 오류. 계정이 잠겼다. 고객센터 통화 후 다시 시도하란다.

다른 가족들에게는 말하지 않았다. 다음 문자메시지가 올지 모른다는 생각이 들어서였다. 하지만 그날 내내 아버지는 카드를 사용하지 않았고 다음 날 고객센터와의 지난한 통화 끝에 로그인해서 결제내역을 보니 삼거리식당은 광명에 있었다. 우리 가족은 광명에 살았던

want to break my promise by fussing about the card that Father was not even using.

It was on Sunday morning, which was the day after we had the second family meeting, when I received a text message on my cell phone:

'web dispatch credit card approved 4,500 won lump-sum payment 12/11 09:11 Samgori Eatery Cumulation 4,500 won'

Not fully awake, I checked the message and thought it was spam. Irritated, I tossed the phone down and was about to turn over when it suddenly occurred to me: 'It's Father! The record of Father's card payment has just been sent to my cell phone.' In a flash, blood rushed to my head and my eyes smarted. I first thought I would call the eldest brother, but while searching the directory for his phone number, I had second thoughts and stopped myself: 'I've got to stay calm. Father knows that each time he uses the card, a text message is sent to my cell phone.' When I received the text regarding a bill payment at an orthopedics clinic, I called Father to ask if he had been injured:

"We now receive a text message right after each credit card payment. Since it's my card, the texts are sent to me."

"Does that mean that you've been receiving texts all along? My goodness! I can't even use the card without minding my daughter," he laughed, but he

적이 없고 아버지의 직장이 광명이었던 적도 없고 친척 중에도 광명 사는 사람은 없다. 전화를 걸어 보니 국밥류를 주로 파는 평범한 식당이었다. 사천오백 원짜리 메뉴는 콩나물국밥이며 인근의 재래시장 사람들이 혼자 와서 아침을 사먹는 경우가 많고 어제 아침에 혼자 콩나물국밥 한 그릇을 먹은 남자 손님은 셀 수도 없다고 한다.

다음 문자메시지는 한 달 후에 왔다. 홍대 앞 커피 전문점에서 이만 이천 원. 토요일 오후였고 나는 광화문에서 영화를 보고 있었다. 문자를 받고는 순간 멍해졌다. 너무 당황스럽고 이상해서 한참 휴대폰 화면을 들여다보다가 겨우 정신을 차렸다. 그 커피 전문점은 커피를 주문하면서 결제하는 곳이다. 이만 이천 원이라면 한 잔이 아니다. 음료와 디저트를 함께 주문했을 수도 있다. 그렇다면 아버지는 아직 홍대의 커피 전문점에 있을지도 모른다. 나는 남자친구의 귀에 "미안, 먼저 갈게"라고 작게 말하고는 대답을 들을 겨를도 없이 상영관을 빠져나와 택시를 잡았다.

토요일 오후의 도로에는 차가 너무 많았다. 막히지 않을 때는 이십 분 정도면 도착할 수 있는 거리인데 금화

used the card again a few days later.

I was certain that this time again, it was Father himself using the card, not a case of a lost card or an act of crime. Even when he knew that I would receive the text, he payed 4,500 won for his break-fast with the card anyway. Why did he do that?

I opened my laptop and searched the Internet for "Samgori Eatery." There were so many eateries with the same name across the country, all of which sold knife-cut noodles, spareribs, soy sauce-sea-soned cutlas fish, and chicken boiled with rice. I wanted to log in my account on the credit card company's homepage, but couldn't remember my code number. I tried and failed to log in once, twice, three times, and after the fourth incorrect code, a guide message asked me to enter my resi-dent registration number as well. I followed the in-struction, but failed to log in twice more and was warned that my account would be locked with one more mistake. I called the customer services cen-ter, but the only service available on Sundays was for reporting lost or stolen cards.

'Should I just report it as a stolen card? If I did, I might be able to find Father. But once I find Father that way, as if he were a common criminal, what's going to happen to my relationship with him? What will become of my family?' I also thought about providing the police with the records of the card payments. 'Would the police quickly find out and

터널을 지날 때 이미 택시에 탄 지 삼십 분이 넘었다. 택시 바닥을 발끝으로 톡톡톡톡 두드리며 어쩔 줄 몰라 하는 나를 룸미러로 흘끔 보더니 기사님이 약속에 많이 늦었느냐고 물었다. 나는 아버지를 찾아야 한다고 불쑥 뱉어놓고 뭐라 말을 잇지 못하고 있었다.

"에이그, 아버님이 치매신가보네? 내가 얼른 갈게요."

기사님은 그냥 요양원에 보내라고, 괜히 가족들 지치고 병난다고, 그래도 딸이 효녀라고 알지도 못하면서 이런저런 말들을 덧붙였고 나는 갑자기 눈물이 터졌다. 고개를 푹 숙이고 두 손으로 얼굴을 가린 채 끅끅 소리를 내며 도착할 때까지 울었다.

커다란 통유리창 너머 바로 보이는 바 좌석에는 빈자리가 하나도 없었다. 대부분 각자의 노트북이나 책을 보고 있고 출입문 옆에 앉은 남자 하나만 멍하니 창밖을 보고 있었다. 아버지는 보이지 않았다. 벽돌로 쌓아올린 계단에 한 발 한 발 디딜 때마다 다리가 부들부들 떨렸다. 문을 열어야 하는데 팔에 힘이 들어가지 않아 두 손으로 긴 손잡이를 잡고 기대듯 몸의 무게를 실어 밀고 들어갔다. 주문하려고 줄을 선 서너 명 중에도 아버지는 없었다.

rush to the location where the card has been used? Do they even have the authority or capability to do so?' I could not trust the police.

I took out a memo pad and made a list of all the code numbers that I had ever used and then crossed out six among them, with which I had already tried and failed. Next, I crossed out the new ones made recently as well as those much too simple. In the end, only two of them were left. After debating for a while, I keyed in one of them. Immediately, with the message 'Incorrect Code Number,' my account got locked down. I was asked to call the customer services center first, then try again.

I decided not to tell the others about it, thinking that I might receive another text soon. But all day long, Father never used the card again. The following day, after an extremely difficult phone conversation with the customer services center, I was able to log in and found out that particular Samgori Eatery was located in Kwangmyong. My family had never lived in Kwangmyong; Father had never worked in Kwangmyong; none of our relatives lived in Kwangmyong. It was just an ordinary eatery with rice-in-soup as its main menu. The 4,500-won meal was rice-in-bean-sprout-soup. It was mostly frequented by the people from the nearby traditional market, most of whom came alone to eat breakfast there. On the previous morning, as usual, so many men came alone and ate rice-in-bean-

목을 있는 대로 빼고 두리번거리며 이층으로 올라갔
다. 좌석은 거의 다 찼고 대체로 내 또래의 젊은 사람들
이었다. 그런데 창가 구석 자리에 희끗한 단발머리를
깔끔하게 넘겨 손질한 할머니가 허리를 세우고 반듯하
게 앉아 있었다. 맞은편에는 털모자를 쓴 어깨가 좁은
남자의 뒷모습. 심장이 두근거렸다. 나도 모르게 몸을
조금 낮추어 두 사람 쪽으로 다가갔다. 주로 할머니가
이야기하고 남자는 고개를 끄덕였는데 음악 소리 때문
인지 내가 제정신이 아니라서 그랬는지 대화 내용은 전
혀 귀에 들어오지 않았다. 테이블 위에는 샌드위치 포
장지와 접시, 포크, 일회용 음료컵 두 개. 심장이 몸을
뚫고 나올 것처럼 너무 쿵쾅거려서 나는 오른손으로 왼
쪽가슴을 지그시 누르면서 걸었다. 드디어, 덜덜 떨리
는 손을 뻗어 남자의 어깨를 툭 밀었다.

"누구세요?"

돌아본 남자는 아버지가 아니었다. 가까이서 보니 두
사람 모두 아버지보다 열 살은 젊어보였다.

"제가 착각을……."

죄송하다는 말도 못하고 황급히 돌아섰다. 노년 커플
에게 다가갈 때보다 더 쿵쾅거리는 가슴을 주먹으로 통

sprout-soup.

The next text came a month later: a charge of 22,000 won at a coffee shop in front of Hong'ik University. On that Saturday afternoon, I was watching a movie at kwanghwa'mun. I was stunned the instant I read the text. The message was so bewildering and extraordinary that I stared at my cell phone for a long time before I finally came around. At that coffee shop, one was supposed to make payment upon order. The amount of 22,000 won meant that the order was more than a cup of coffee. A drink could have been ordered together with some dessert. If so, Father might still be at the coffee shop near Hong'ik University. I whispered to my boyfriend, "I'm sorry, but I've got to leave now," and without waiting for his response, I rushed out of the movie theater and took a taxi.

As on any other Saturday afternoon, there were too many cars on the roads. If there were no traffic jam, it would take only twenty minutes or so to get to the coffee shop. But by the time the taxi was running through Kumhwa Tunnel, I had already spent longer than half an hour in the taxi. I kept stamping the tips of my feet on the floor impatiently. Throwing a glance at me in the mirror, the driver asked me if I was very late for my appointment. I blurted out that I had to find my father, but then I did not know what else to say to him.

"Oh no! Your father has dementia, hasn't he?

통 치며 이층 테이블을 하나하나 둘러보았다. 나를 둘러싼 모든 얼굴들이 낯설다는 것이 이렇게 큰 공포일 줄은 몰랐다. 휴대폰을 꺼내 보니 결제문자가 도착한 지 벌써 한 시간이 다 되었다. 그 사이 남자친구가 전화를 여섯 번 했고 메시지를 두 개 보냈다. 걱정되니 연락 달라는 내용이었다.

일층으로 내려가 다시 한 바퀴 둘러보고 아이스 아메리카노를 주문했다. 주문을 받는 알바생에게 휴대폰에 저장되어 있던 아버지 사진을 보여주며 한 시간쯤 전에 여기서 이만 이천 원을 결제했다고, 혹시 기억이 나느냐고 물었다. 그녀는 이십 분 전부터 아르바이트를 시작했다며 이전 타임 알바생은 이미 집에 갔다고 대답했다.

"무슨 일이신지 모르지만 시시티브이 보고 싶으시면 일단 경찰에 신고하셔야 해요."

머리가 쨍할 정도로 차가운 아메리카노를 단숨에 들이켰다. 아버지는 대체 누구와 여기서 이만 이천 원어치를 샀을까. 한동안 단발머리 할머니의 얼굴이 머릿속에서 떠나지 않았다.

아버지는 돌아오지 않고 오빠들과 나는 예전보다 자

Don't worry, I'll step on it."

The driver went on to suggest that we should send my father to a home, otherwise the rest of the family would be tired out and get sick. Knowing nothing about the real situation, he continued saying this and that, including his observation that at least I was a filial daughter. I ended up bursting into tears. With my head deeply bowed and my face buried in my hands, I could not stop sobbing until I arrived at the coffee shop.

Inside the large picture window, I could see no vacant seats at the bar table. Most of the customers were either staring at their laptop screens or reading books, except for the man sitting near the entrance door who was looking out the window absently. Father was nowhere to be seen from the outside. Taking one step after another up the brick stairs, I felt my legs shaking uncontrollably. My arms also felt so weak that I held onto the long door handle with both hands, then leaned over and pushed the door open, using my body weight. There were three or four people standing in a line to make orders, but Father was not there, either.

I walked up to the second floor, craning out my neck and looking around for Father. Almost all the seats were taken mainly by young people of my age. Suddenly I spotted a grandmother sitting up square at a table by the window in one corner of the hall. Her back was straight and her short, gray

주 엄마만 있는 집에 들른다. 올케언니와 조카들까지 모두 오는 주말도 있고 조카들만 따라오는 주말도 있고 삼남매만 오붓하게 모이는 주말도 있다. 열심히 음식을 차리던 엄마는 이제 음식 재료들만 사다 놓는다. 함께 김치전을 부쳐 먹고 삼겹살을 구워 먹고 만두를 빚어 먹었다. 작은오빠가 만두를 너무 예쁘게 잘 빚어서 놀랐다. 식사가 끝나면 오빠들이 싱크대에 나란히 서서 한 명은 세제 묻힌 수세미로 그릇을 닦고 또 한 명은 헹궈내어 설거지까지 깔끔하게 마쳤다. 내가 우리 오빠들 같지가 않다고 하자 올케언니가 집에서는 많이 한다고 말했다.

"요리, 설거지, 청소, 빨래, 다 잘 해요. 근데 이상하게 이 집 대문만 통과하면 무슨 다른 차원으로 넘어 온 것처럼 아무 것도 안 하고 바닥에 척 들러붙더라고요."

아차 싶었는지 언니가 옆 눈으로 엄마를 한 번 스윽 봤다. 엄마는 그럼, 요즘 세상에 다 같이 해야지, 하며 고개를 끄덕였다. 엄마가 그렇게 생각할 줄은 몰랐다. 다 같이 해야 하는 요즘 세상에도 엄마는 모든 집안일을 당연하고 자연스럽게 자신의 일로 받아들이며 평생 혼자 했다.

hair was neatly swept back. A narrow-shouldered man with a woolen cap on was sitting opposite her. My heartbeat quickened. Since I could see only the man's back from where I was, I moved towards them, involuntarily bending down a little. The grandmother was talking most of the time and the man was silently nodding his head. Perhaps because of the music or because I was not in my right mind at the time, I could not make out what they were talking about. On the table were some sandwich wrappings, a dish, forks, and two paper cups. As my heart was pounding hard as if it would burst out of my chest, I walked with my right hand gently pressed on my chest. At last, I stretched out my badly trembling hand and gave the man a light push on the shoulder.

"Who are you?"

The man turned his head, but he was not my father. From up close, both of them looked about ten years younger than my father.

"Ah, I mistook you for . . ."

I hastily turned around and left them, unable even to say sorry. Rapping on my chest with my fist now because my heart was beating even faster, I walked around the second floor to check on all the other tables one by one. I had never known how dreadful it is to be surrounded by many unfamiliar faces. I took out my cell phone; it had already been almost an hour since the arrival of the text. During

"엄마는 살림이 천성인 줄 알았더니."

"천성은 개뿔. 아주 징글징글하다."

함께 음식을 해 먹는 시간이 많아지며 우리는 서로에
대해 더 잘 알게 되었다. 큰오빠에게는 제과제빵 자격
증이 있다. 빵을 직접 구워 파는 작은 베이커리 겸 카페
를 차리는 게 큰오빠의 꿈이다. 지금은 그저 막연하게
생각하고 있지만 사업 자금이 모이는 대로 시작할 거라
고, 올케언니도 동의하고 같이 준비하고 있다고 한다.
작은오빠네가 불임클리닉을 다녔다는 사실도 알게 되
었다. 첫째는 아무 어려움 없이 낳았는데 둘째가 생기
지 않아 마음고생을 많이 한 모양이다. 부부는 그냥 하
나만 잘 키우기로 결정했는데 주변에서 자꾸 왜 둘째를
낳지 않느냐, 하나는 외롭다는 소리를 해서 답답하단
다. 종종 그런 말을 했던 엄마가 오빠에게 사과했다. 문
자 한 번 주고받지 않던 삼남매의 단체 대화방이 생겼
다. 돌아가며 매일 저녁 엄마에게 안부 전화를 하게 됐
다. 나는 남자친구와 헤어졌고 승진했고 월세 계약을
이 년 연장했다.

문자메시지도 드물게, 하지만 계속 온다. 왕십리의 노
래방에서 만 이천 원, 파주의 아울렛에서 오만 팔천 원,

the hour, my boyfriend had called me six times and sent two text messages, asking me to call him back since he was worried.

I went down to the main floor and after looking around at the people there once more, I ordered a glass of iced Americano. And showing my father's picture stored in my cell phone to the part-time worker who took my order, I told her that about an hour before, he had made a payment of 22,000 won with a credit card, and asked if she remembered seeing him. She answered that she had been working only for twenty minutes, replacing the previous shift who had already gone home.

"I don't know what this is all about, but if you want to see the CCTV, you must report it to the police first."

I gulped down the iced Americano that was cold enough to give me a brief brain freeze. 'Father and someone else have bought 22,000 won's worth of food here. Who on earth is the other person?' For quite a while, the face of the grandmother with short hair lingered in my mind.

Father has not returned yet, so my brothers and I visit, more often than before, our parents' house where Mother lives alone now. Some weekends, sisters-in-law and nephews join us; some other weekends, only nephews do. There are weekends, of course, only the three of us siblings come together and visit with Mother. Although she used to

지리산 입구의 밥집에서 만 육천 원, 제주도의 횟집에서 십이만 사천 원……. 처음에는 문자메시지를 받자마자 택시를 타고 결제한 곳으로 달려가곤 했다. 아버지는 이미 없고 아르바이트생도 손님들도 아버지를 제대로 기억해내지 못했다. 몇 차례 허탕을 친 후에는 메시지를 받고도 달려가지 않게 되었다.

남들이 들으면 미쳤다고 하겠지만 나는 그게 아버지가 보내는 메시지인 것 같다. 나는 잘 지내고 있다. 이곳은 경치가 좋구나. 너무 걱정 마라. 엄마에게 말하지 마라. 지리산을 오르고 제주 바다를 구경하고 테이크아웃 커피를 마시며 젊은 사람들이 많은 거리를 걷는 아버지를 생각한다. 미안하지만 아버지 없이도 남은 가족들은 잘 살고 있다. 아버지도 가족을 떠나 잘 살고 있는 듯하다. 그래서 언젠가 아버지가 다시 돌아오면 아무 일 없다는 듯 예전처럼 지낼 수 있을 것 같다.

work so hard preparing meals for us, Mother does only grocery shopping now. All of us then make *kimchi* pancakes, grill sliced pork belly, and make dumplings together. I was surprised to see the second elder brother make such pretty dumplings. After the meal, the brothers do the dishes together, standing side by side at the kitchen sink; one sponge-soaps the dishes while the other rinses them clean. When I once said they did not seem to be the brothers that I had known, the older sister-in-law said my brother quite often helped out with the dishes at home.

"He cooks, does the dishes, vacuums, washes clothes, and he's quite good at them, too. But for some strange reason, once he walks through the front gate of this house, he behaves as if he were in a different world, just lying around doing nothing, as if he'd become one with the floor."

She then flinched, doing a double take, and stole a sidelong glance at my mother. Mother nodded and said, "Of course, in this day and age, you should help each other." I never expected Mother would think that way. Even in this day and age when we all should help one another, Mother has been doing all the chores by herself throughout her life, accepting it as her most natural and inevitable duty.

"I always thought Mother is a good housekeeper by nature."

"By nature? Heck no! I'm sick of it."

The more often we cook and eat together, the better we get to know one another. The eldest brother has patisserie's and baker's certificates. His dream is to open a small bakery-cum-caf where he can bake and sell pastry and bread. He is only thinking about it now, but as soon as he has enough money saved, he will put it into practice. His wife agrees to his plan and they are preparing for it together. Now I also know that the second elder brother and his wife have visited infertility clinics. They had no problem having the first child, but since then, they have not been able to have a second one. They were heartbroken before, of course, but now they are determined to be content with raising their only child well. But then those around the couple keep saying that they should have another child, otherwise the first child will be too lonely. Whenever they hear it, they feel frustrated. Mother who often said the same has apologized to the brother. The three of us, who have never exchanged any text messages, now have a group chat room. Moreover, we take turns giving Mother a phone call every evening to check if she is all right. I have broken up with my boyfriend, been promoted, and extended the rental contract of my place another two years.

The text messages of the card payments are still coming, though rarely: 12,000 won at a *karaoke* room in Wangshimni, 58,000 won at an outlet in

Paju, 16,000 won at an eatery at the approach to Jiri Mountain, 124,000 won at a raw fish restaurant on Jeju Island . . . I used to race to the place of the card payment by taxi as soon as the message arrived. But each time, Father had already left the place, and neither the part-time workers nor the other customers remembered Father clearly. After several failed attempts, though, I stopped hastening to the places even after I received messages.

Some people, if they hear me saying so, will call me crazy, but I believe the text messages are Father's way of letting us know how he is doing: "I'm doing fine. It's beautiful here. Don't worry about me. Don't tell your mom." I think of my father climbing Jiri Mountain, gazing out to the sea surrounding Jeju Island, drinking takeout coffee and walking the streets crowded with young people. I am sorry to say this, but even without Father, the rest of us are doing just fine. Father also seems to be doing all right away from his family. So, when he returns home someday, I believe, we will be able to get along well together as we used to, as if nothing had ever happened.

창작노트
Writer's Note

제 노트북에는 '가출'이라는 이름이 붙은 파일이 두 개 있습니다. '가출2010.hwp'와 '창비_가출.hwp'입니다. 2010년에 썼던 소설을 오래 두고 다시 고쳐《창작과비평》2018년 봄호에 발표한 것입니다. '아버지가 가출했다'는 문장을 처음 쓴 것은 2010년 11월 2일 밤이었고 정확히 그 한 달 전인 2010년 10월 2일에 아버지가 돌아가셨습니다.

각자의 생활에 바빠 자주 만나지 못했던 가족, 친지들이 장례식을 위해 모이고 내내 함께 시간을 보냈는데 정작 우리를 불러 모은 아버지가 안 계신 상황이 기묘하기도 했고 괴롭기도 했습니다. 낯설고 복잡한 장례

There are two files named "Run Away" stored in my laptop: "Run Away 2010.hwp" and "Changbi_Run Away.hwp." I wrote the first story in 2010 and after having gone through a long process of revision, published the second one in the spring issue of 2018 Changjak kwa Pi'pyong. The opening sentence of the story, "Father's run away from home," was first written on the night of November 2, 2010, which was exactly a month after my own father passed away on October 2, 2010.

The remaining members of my family and relatives, who had been too busy to get together often, came to the funeral and spent some time together. But it was strange as well as painful to

절차들을 모두 마치고 나서야 여러 감정들이 걷잡을 수 없게 올라왔고 정리되지 않은 채로 소설을 썼습니다.

초고에는 죄책감과 후회, 의문, 원망, 피로가 거칠게 담겨 있었고 소설이라고 이름 붙이기 민망할 정도로 제 이야기가 고스란히 적혀 있었습니다. 이후로 한 번씩 파일을 열어서 조금씩 지우고 다시 쓰다가 계간지에 신기 위해 많은 부분을 수정했습니다. 노년의 아버지가 갑자기 가출한 후 딸인 나의 신용카드를 쓴다는 설정 정도만 남았네요. 시간이 흐르면서 제 감정도 정리되고 가족들의 생활도 안정되자 이 경험을 거리를 두고 바라볼 수 있게 된 것 같습니다. '내 아버지가 돌아가신 개인적인 일'이 아니라 '가부장의 부재'로 생각해 보려고 했습니다.

가부장 문화는 사회 구성원들의 가치관이 변하고 개별 가정의 모습이 다양해지고 그런 변화가 세대를 거쳐 이어져 내려온 후에야 아마도 조금씩 느리게 사라질 거라고 생각해왔습니다. 상황을 뒤집어보고 싶었습니다. 어떤 이유이건 한순간 가부장 문화가 사라진다면 가정의 분위기는 어떻게 될까. 구성원들의 가치관과 태도는 어떻게 달라질까. 그래서 가부장이 없는 가정, 아버지

realize my father was no longer among us and yet he was the one who had convened all of us there. Only after all the unfamiliar and complicated funeral procedures were over, I felt many different emotions surging up uncontrollably within me. The story was written while those emotions were still raw and yet to be sorted out.

The first draft contained a mixture of unfiltered feelings of guilt, regret, doubt, resentment, and fatigue narrated in a disorderly fashion. It portrayed myself then so literally that it was even embarrassing to call it a work of fiction.

Afterwards, I would open the file every now and then and revise it little by little. When it was chosen to be published in the quarterly, I revised many more parts of the manuscript. All that still remains from the first draft is the setup that the aged father suddenly runs away from home and uses his daughter's, that is, the "I"'s credit card. It seems that with the passage of time, my emotions became settled and the lives of family members gained stability, which in turn enabled me to distance myself from the experience. I then attempted a thematic change from 'my father's death as a personal experience' to 'the absence of patriarch.'

Patriarchy, I always thought, would probably dis-

가 사라진 가정의 이야기를 쓰게 되었습니다. 이번에도 역시나 멋없고 직설적인 소설이 되었고요.

권위적인 아버지들이 문제라거나 아버지 때문에 가족들이 불행하다고 말하려던 것은 아닙니다. 이 지독한 가부장 문화는 누구를 행복하게, 혹은 불행하게 하는지 묻고 싶었습니다. 소설을 쓰며 제가 얻은 답은 소설의 결말과 같습니다.

소설을 쓰는 일은 매번 다르게 어렵습니다. 이번에는 이야기에서 거리를 두는 일이 꼭 필요했고 어려웠습니다. 소설 속 '나'는 내가 아니고 소설 속 '아버지'는 내 아버지가 아니라고 계속 되뇌었고 그래서인지 오래 지니며 고쳐왔는데도 마냥 소중하고 애틋하지 않고 오히려 조금 불편한 감정이 있습니다. 애증의 소설이랄까요.

인쇄된 소설을 읽고 관련해 인터뷰를 하고 이렇게 창작노트를 쓰면서 자연스럽고 편안하게 아버지 생각을 할 수 있었습니다. 감사한 일입니다. 이 소설도, 창작노트도 읽으실 수 없겠지만 아버지께 같은 대답을 들려드리고 싶습니다. 남은 가족들은 잘 살고 있다고. 아버지도 잘 지내실 거라고 생각한다고.

appear slowly little by little through a long period of time and many generations, as the value systems held by the members of society change and all families come to have their individual shapes and characteristics. At some point, however, it occurred to me to give a twist to such a perspective of mine. If the system of patriarchy, for whatever reason, suddenly disappeared, how would the family members feel about the change? How would their values and behavior change? This is how the story of a family with their father, that is, the patriarch gone came about. And this time again, I ended up producing a rather dry and outspoken narrative.

I never intended, though, to say that the authoritative father is problematic or that the father makes the other family members feel unhappy. I just wanted to ask whom this staunch culture of patriarchy makes happy or unhappy. The answer I got in the course of writing the story is the same as its ending.

Writing works of fiction is difficult and each one differently so. This time, it was essential for me to detach myself from the story even while writing it, and that was very difficult. I kept repeating to myself that the "I" in the story was not me and "Father" in the story was not my father. Probably that is why even after having kept it close at hand through the long process of revision, the story does not feel all that precious or dear to my heart; instead, there lingers a sense of discomfort. Perhaps, I could call it a love-hate relationship.

Reading the story after its publication, giving interviews on it, writing this note, I have been able to think of my father in a natural and peaceful way.

For that, I am grateful. My father can read neither the story nor this writer's note, but I would like to say to my father: "The rest of us are doing just fine, and I believe you are fine as well."

해설
Commentary

가족이라는 현실적인 판타지

노태훈 (문학평론가)

오늘날 페미니즘의 물결은 한국문학을 완전히 새롭게 뒤바꿔놓고 있다고 해도 과언이 아니고, 그 기폭제가 『82년생 김지영』(민음사, 2016)이었음은 새삼스러운 언급일 것이다. 비단 한국의 상황만 그러한 것은 아니겠지만 이제 작가들은 젠더 감수성을 배제한 채 소설을 쓰기 어려워졌고, 독자들은 작품에 나타나는 불평등하고 차별적인 젠더 인식을 더 이상 참아주지 않는다. 그러나 모든 예술이 그렇듯이 소설은 무작정 유토피아를 그려내는 장르가 아니며, 오히려 우리가 현실 속에서 마주하는 차별과 혐오를 더욱 집요하게, 또 날카롭게 묘사하지 않으면 안 된다. 이럴 때 작가와 독자의 욕망은 같아진다. 무엇이 문제인지 정확하게 알고 싶다는 것, 또 가능

Family: A Realistic Fantasy

Roh Tae-hoon (Literary critic)

The recent tide of feminism is causing drastic changes in Korean literature. Needless to say, it was triggered by *Chi-yong Kim born in 1982* (Seoul: Min'umsa, 2016) written by Nam-ju Cho. Writers now find it hard to produce works without being sensitive to the gender issues; and readers themselves no longer tolerate the unequal, discriminating gender representations they find in the works of fiction. Probably these changes are not limited to Korea. Nevertheless, as is true in all artistic creations, the genre of fiction is not meant to blindly portray utopias; but to describe the discrimination and hatred we face in reality more keenly and persistently. Only then, the writer and the reader come to share the same desire to know what exactly is the

하다면 그 문제를 해결할 방법을 찾고 싶다는 것.

하지만 성차별의 역사는 사실상 인류 역사 전체라고 봐야 할 것이고, 이 세계의 어떤 관념도 그처럼 견고하게 형성되어 오지는 않았다. 게다가 젠더로서의 여성을 하나의 고정된 정체성으로 간주하기에 개별 여성 주체들은 너무도 다양한 조건과 복잡한 상황에 놓여져 있다. 그리고 여성의 문제는 우리가 미처 문제라고 인식하지 못했을 뿐 이미 잘 알고 있는 현실이어서 단순히 그것을 재현하는 것만으로는 그러한 페미니즘 서사의 목표를 달성하기 어렵다. 그럼에도 불구하고 지금 한국의 여성 작가들은 각자 다양한 방식을 통해 성공적인 페미니즘 서사를 구현해내고 있는데, 조남주의 경우 여성 인물을 통해 혼인과 혈연으로 이어진 가족이라는 공동체를 지속적으로 문제 삼고 있다는 점이 큰 호응을 얻고 있다.

"차라리 출가했다고 하면 믿었을" 72세 아버지의 '가출' 소식으로 시작하는 이 소설은 이제는 그 폐해에 대해 이견을 제시하기는 어려울 가부장제를 다룬다. "일곱 살이나 어린 아내에게 꼬박꼬박 존댓말을 쓰는 아버지. 그렇지만 엄마가 숟가락과 젓가락과 마실 물까지 완벽하게 제자리에 놓아야 식탁에 와 앉는 아버지. 정

problem and if possible, to find a solution.

In fact, the history of gender discrimination is coeval with the history of humanity itself; and no other ideology in the world has been as firmly built and maintained as gender inequality. Further, all women as a gender are considered to have one fixed identity, so individual female subjects find themselves forced into many different conditions and complex situations. As a matter of fact, women's problems are well-known realities, though they have not been recognized as such yet; so, simply reproducing them will not help achieve the objective of the feminist discourse. Nevertheless, the women writers in Korea are now generating successful feminist narrations in their own ways; and Nam-ju Cho, for one, is earning a great response by creating female characters who keep bringing into question the family as a community whose members are tied together by blood and marriage.

"Ga'chul" or "Run Away" begins with the news of a seventy-two-year-old father's 'running away from home,' which the "I" (or the narrator) "would have believed" if it were not *ga'chul* but *chulga*, that is, if "Father had become a Buddhist priest." The story deals with the system of patriarchy, the harmful effect of which is no longer defensible.

년까지 근무하는 동안 양가 부모님 장례 이외에는 한 번도 결근한 적이 없는, 삼남매가 태어나던 날도 출근했다는 아버지. 눈에 보이지 않는 것은 믿지 않는다며 신용카드도 만들지 않고 자동이체도 하지 않고 인터넷뱅킹도 하지 않는 아버지"라는 한 단락에서 우리는 본인이 살아온 방식에 대해 어떠한 변화의 여지도 주지 않는, 고집스러운 각자의 아버지를 떠올리게 된다. 그것이 옳으냐 그르냐를 떠나 자신이 체득한 삶의 양식을 절대 양보하지 않는 그 오기야말로 한국의 전형적인 아버지상일 것이다.

그 아버지가 홀연히 자취를 감춘 뒤 남은 가족, 즉 '엄마'와 삼남매가 묘한 활기와 유대감을 느끼는 것 역시 낯선 일이 아니다. 이들 가족이 대책 회의를 위해 모인 식사 자리의 메뉴는 "청국장"이었는데, 삼남매 모두가 어려서부터 좋아했던 그 청국장은 아버지가 싫어하는 바람에 "아버지가 야근하시는 날"에야 겨우 먹을 수 있던 것이었다. 요컨대 아버지가 '부재'해야만 가능했던 일들과 분위기가 있다는 것인데, 할아버지가 없다는 것을 눈치챈 '나'의 조카들이 신나게 할아버지의 방을 어질러 놓고 노는 것처럼 어쩌면 그것은 거의 본능적인

Father always uses the polite speech with Mother who is seven years younger than him. And yet, he will never come to sit at the dining table until Mother finishes setting the table perfectly with spoons, chopsticks, and glasses of water all in place. He never missed a day of work until he retired, except for the funeral days of his and Mother's parents. He went to work even on the day each of his three children was born. Insisting that he does not trust anything he cannot see with his own eyes, he refuses to get credit cards, wire-transfer money, or use the Internet-banking.

The paragraph quoted above reminds us of our own stubborn fathers who will allow no room for change in the ways they have lived their lives. Whether it is right or wrong, they absolutely refuse to give up the lifestyle that they have acquired and mastered. This unyieldingness is indeed the image of the typical Korean father.

Such a father suddenly disappears from home and the remaining family, that is, 'Mother' and her three grown-up children feel a surge of vitality and a stronger familial bond within and among themselves, which may be inexplicable, yet is not at all unfamiliar. When the children come to their parents' house to discuss what to do about their fa-

감각일지 모른다.

아버지가 사라진 자리에 당연히 남는 것은 '엄마'이다. 남편이 가출한 지 한 달이 되어서야 겨우 '딸'에게 연락한 '엄마'는 자식들을 소환해 "밥부터" 차린다. 그리고 모인 삼남매는 너무도 자연스럽게 또 맛있게 그 밥을 먹는다. 가족이라면 모름지기 한 밥상에서 같은 음식을 먹어야 한다는, 즉 '식구(食口)'여야 한다는 인식은 한국 사회의 뿌리 깊은 문화라고 봐야 할 것이다. 아버지의 문제로 매주 모여 "함께 음식을 해 먹는 시간이 많아지며 우리는 서로에 대해 더 잘 알게 되었다"고 '나'가 말하는 것처럼, 조남주는 가족이 곧 식구라는 인식을 부정하지 않는다. 다만 여기에서 놓치지 말아야 할 점은 그 음식을 "함께" 만들고, 먹고, 정리한다는 것이다.

'엄마'가 살림이 "아주 징글징글"하다고 말하면서, '오빠들'이 음식을 만들고 설거지를 하는 풍경은 아버지가 사라진 뒤에야 비로소 가능해진다. 이런 분위기에서는 '엄마'도 자신의 목소리를 낸다. 늘 아버지가 말하고, 결정하는 동안 '엄마'는 그저 "중얼거리는 사람"이었는데, '나'는 그제야 엄마의 말을 분명히 듣고 "발음이 너무 좋았다"는 사실을 깨닫는다. 이런 '엄마'의 소외에는 '아버

ther's disappearance, the mother prepares dinner for them, including *chong'gukjang*. All three of the children have always loved to eat *chong'gukjang* since their childhood, but because the father hated it, they could eat it "only when Father was on night duty." The gist here is that some things or atmospheres are available for them to enjoy only when the father is 'absent.' Perhaps people feel it almost instinctively as is evident in the scene where the "I"'s little nephews, taking notice that their grandfather is gone, have so much fun playing in his room, making a mess of it.

The father's departure leaves 'Mother' all alone in the house. She waits as long as a whole month after her husband's *ga'chul* before she tells her 'daughter' about it. The first thing 'Mother' does, while waiting for her children to come to her house, is prepare "dinner" for them. The three children then fully enjoy the meal as if it is a most natural thing to do. According to the time-honored cultural tradition of Korea, it is proper that a family should sit together at the same table and share the food. Hence shik'gu, the Korean equivalent of "family," meaning "those who eat together." The remaining family members in this story also share food once a week when they get together to dis-

지'의 경제권 독점이 가장 큰 영향력을 행사했음을 작가는 지적하고 있다. 막스 베버가 가부장제의 확장된 형태의 하나로 "가산제(patrimonialism)"의 개념을 제시했듯, '아버지'는 온갖 공과금마저도 "그건 내 일"이라고 말하면서 자본 통제의 방식으로 가족주의를 형성해왔던 것이다. '나'에게 독립을 마지못해 허락하면서 "결혼 자금에 보태려고 모아두었다는 3천만원 통장"을 내미는 모습 역시 전형적인 가부장적 가산제의 형태이다.

이런 방식의 가족주의는 한국 사회의 일반적인 모습이기도 한데, 그것을 단적으로 보여주는 것이 태생과 성별에 따라 역할 분담과 대우를 달리 받는 삼남매의 모습이다. 가장 먼저 태어난 남성에게는 '장남', 두 번째로 태어난 남성에게는 '차남', 그리고 세 번째로 태어난 딸에게는 '막내'라는 호칭을 부여하고, 이 보통명사는 차별의 근거가 된다. '아버지'와의 관계에서는 '역할'로만 존재하던 이들 삼남매가 아버지의 가출 후 그 이름표를 떼어버리고 각자의 고민을 나누는 모습은 가부장제가 가족 공동체 형성에 얼마나 큰 장애물인지를 증명하는 장면이라고 볼 수 있는데, 특히 살가운 막내딸로서의 '나'가 아버지와 겪었던 갈등은 그러한 역할과 기대 때문

cuss the father's disappearance; and the "I" says, "the more often we cook and eat together, the better we get to know one another." Obviously, Nam-ju Cho does not deny the notion that a family is *shik'gu*. However, we should not overlook one important point here: all of them cook, eat, and clean up "together."

Only after the father's disappearance, it becomes possible for 'Mother' to confess she is "sick of housekeeping" and for the "I"'s brothers to volunteer to cook and do the dishes. In this changed atmosphere, 'Mother' can speak her mind. The father has always been the speaker and decision maker for the family while 'Mother' has remained simply a "mumbler." But now, the "I" can hear her mother's voice clearly and realizes 'Mother' is capable of making "such concise sentences and clear pronunciations." The writer makes it plain that behind the isolation of 'Mother' was mainly 'Father' monopolizing the family finances. As Max Weber put forward the concept of "patrimonialism" as one of the extended forms of patriarchy, 'Father' has maintained the ideology of familism by means of capital control, declaring even paying public utility bills "his job, and no one else's." Reluctantly allowing the "I" to move out of his house, the father "handed me a

이었다. 그럼에도 불구하고 결국 아버지, 엄마 모두와 가장 가까이에서 일상을 공유하는 존재가 '나'라는 점은 가족 공동체에서 여성이 갖는 위치를 여실히 보여준다. 실제로 이 소설에서 아버지의 가출 이후 '오빠들'은 그다지 적극적인 모습을 보여주지 못하고, 오로지 '나'만이 아버지의 카드 사용 내역을 가끔 문자메시지로 확인하면서 이 사태를 주도적으로 바라보고 있다. 그것은 우리로 하여금 가부장, 즉 남성이 아니라 여성이라는 젠더가 가족 공동체의 중심임을 명확히 인식하게 만든다.

우리는 조남주의 「가출」을 리얼리티 서사로 읽어서는 곤란할 것 같다. 아버지의 가출 이후 이 가족은 아버지를 찾기 위해 노력하기는 하지만 그것이 일상을 지배하지는 않고 오히려 집안은 서서히 안정되어 가는데, '나'가 아닌 다른 가족 구성원의 관점에서는 이해하기 어려운 측면이 있다. 특히 아내인 '엄마'의 남편에 대한 감정이 거의 드러나지 않고, 또 아버지가 집을 나간 이유도 전혀 설명되지 않는다. 즉 이 소설은 살부(殺父)의 서사를 가출이라는 완곡한 방식으로 그려낸 일종의 판타지이다. 그러므로 "미안하지만 아버지 없이도 남은 가족들은 잘살고 있다. 아버지도 가족을 떠나 잘 살고 있는

bankbook with a deposit balance of 30,000,000 won, which he said he had been saving for my wedding." What is depicted in this scene is typically patrimonial as well.

This type of familism, which is widely practiced in Korean society, is most directly displayed in the different treatments and roles given to the three siblings, according to their birth order and gender. The firstborn son is called *jangnam*, and the second son *cha'nam*, and the youngest daughter *mangnae*; and these common nouns provide grounds for discrimination, and the nature of each child's relationship with the father is determined only by his/her given role. However, after the father's disappearance, they strip themselves of their given roles and begin to share their problems among themselves. The scene of their open-hearted communication evinces just how big a barrier patriarchy poses to the formation of the familial community. In particular, the conflict between the "I" and her father is born of the role of a warm-hearted youngest daughter imposed on her and what is expected of her as such. Nevertheless, the "I" is the one who remains closer to both 'Father' and 'Mother' than any other sibling, sharing everyday life with her parents, which clearly demonstrates the posi-

듯하다. 그래서 언젠가 아버지가 다시 돌아오면 아무 일 없다는 듯 예전처럼 지낼 수 있을 것 같다"는 문장으로 소설은 귀결될 수밖에 없다.

조남주는 흔히 '4인 가족'으로 명명되는 정상 가족의 신화를 깨트리려 하면서도, 그것을 아예 해체시키는 방식이 아니라 여전히 가족이라는 공동체가 가지는 가치를 수긍하는 태도를 보여준다. 다시 말해 어떤 형태의 구성원도 가족이 될 수 있다는 다소 추상적인 차원이 아니라 현실적으로 우리가 상상 가능한 이상적 공동체의 형태가 가족일 수밖에 없음을 인정하는 것이다. 어쩌면 이 소설은 신경숙의 『엄마를 부탁해』(창비, 2008)가 10년 뒤에 도달한 지점일지 모른다. 이제 실종되는 것은 엄마가 아니라 아버지이고, 그 부재 속에서 남은 가족들은 절절한 그리움에 빠지는 것이 아니라 비로소 각자의 방식으로 해방된다. 여기에 아버지 역시 스스로의 굴레를 벗어던지고 나름의 자유를 찾는 것으로 그려지고 있으니, 지금 한국의 가족 공동체가 마주한 당면 과제야말로 '가족 리부트'가 아닐까.

노태훈 서울대학교 국어국문학과 졸업 및 동대학원 박사 수료. 2013년 '중앙신인문학상'으로 등단.

tion women take within the familial community. In fact, the brothers in the story, while dealing with the father's disappearance, are not all that earnest. It is only the "I" that takes the leading role in coping with the situation by keeping track of the details of her father's credit card payments via the cell phone text messages that arrive every now and then. This makes us recognize that the center of the familial community is not the patriarch, that is, not the male but the female gender.

We should abstain from reading Nam-ju Cho's "Run Away" as a story narrating realities. After the father leaves home, the family do make an effort to find him; but, it does not become a priority in their daily lives; rather, the family are gradually regaining stability. We the readers are told of this develop- ment only by the "I" and no one else in the family. For example, nothing is told about the mother's feelings towards her husband. Further, the reason for the father's leaving home is not provided at all. In a nutshell, this story is a fantasy depicting patri- cide in a roundabout way. Hence the conclusion:

I am sorry to say this, but even without Father, the rest of us are doing just fine. Father also seems to be doing all right away from his family. So, when he returns home someday, I believe, we will be able to get along well together as we used to, as if nothing has ever happened.

On the one hand, the writer tries to shatter the myth of the normal family, also known as 'a family of four'; on the other, she refrains from completely dismantling it by still approving of the value of the community called "family." In other words, she does not propose the rather abstract argument that a family may come in any form or shape. Instead, she acknowledges that the family may be imagined as an ideal community, but should also be in realistically imaginable forms or shapes. Perhaps, this story is on the same continuum as *Please Look After Mom* (Seoul: Changbi, 2008) that was published ten years earlier. Now, however, it is the father, not the mother, who disappears from home. In the absence of the father, the rest of the family, rather than grieving over their loss, are finally able to free themselves in their individual ways. The father also breaks away from his self-imposed fetter and emancipates himself in his own fashion. If so, the familial communities in Korea may be facing at the moment the task of 'rebooting the family.'

Roh Tae-hoon Roh Tae-hoon received a B.A. in Korean literature from Seoul National University and is currently pursuing a Ph.D. in the same program. He made his literary debut in 2013, when he won the JoongAng New Writer Award.

비평의 목소리
Critical Acclaim

"아버지가 가출했다"는 문장으로 시작하는 조남주의 「가출」은 72세의 아버지가 갑작스럽게 선택한 가출이 야기하는 가족 구성원들의 변화 혹은 성장을 보여주는 소설이다. 한국적 가부장의 삶을 전형적으로, 한편으로는 모범적으로 살아가던 아버지가 돌연히 감행한 가출의 실존적 원인과 이유에 대해 이 소설은 관심을 보이지 않는다. 오히려 이 소설은 아버지의 부재라는 미스테리한 사건 이후의 시간에 남게 된 사람들, 다시 말해 가부장을 중심으로 구성되었던 가족 내 관계의 변화에 초점이 맞춰져 있다.

강동호(Kang Dong-ho), 《이 계절의 소설》 선정이유,
문학과 지성사 홈페이지, 2018

Cho Nam-joo's short story "Run Away," which begins with the powerful sentence "Father's run away from home," tells the story of a family's change and growth after its 72-year-old patriarch has suddenly decided to leave home. The story is not concerned with the possible existential crises or other causes, though, for the actions of this father, who had led the typical and exemplary life a Korean patriarch. Rather, it focuses on the family members who are left to cope with their lives and each other in his mysterious absence, in particular, on the changes in the relationships within the family, which had been organized around its patriarch.

Kang Dong-ho, *Moonji Publishing* (2018)

아버지가 사라지자 남은 사람들은 여느 때처럼 식사를 준비하고 맛있게 먹는다. 이 의례는 점점 자연스러워진다. 또한 아버지가 집 안에 존재하던 시절, 아버지는 '자신의 일'을 부각시키는 데 혈안이 되었지만, 아버지가 사라지자 남은 가족들은 하고 싶었던 '자신의 일'이 무엇이었는지 생각을 주고받는다. 특히 아버지가 사라진 뒤 딸은 아들은 엄마는 자신이 꿈꾸고 설계했던 생애가 무엇이었는지 입 밖으로 꺼내기 시작한다. 어쩌면 「가출」은 자기실종을 택할 수밖에 없는 경제인간으로서의 남성과 그 비극을 주시하는 소설이 아니라, 가장으로 온화하게 '군림'했던 남성이 부재했을 때 남은 가족들에게 다시 찾아온 '생애 전망'의 희망을 말하는 소설이 아닐까.

김신식(Kim Shin-sik), 「탈존인가 폐존인가: '출가외인'의 사회학」, 《이 계절의 소설》 선정이유, 문학과 지성사 홈페이지, 2018

After the father disappears, the remaining family members prepare meals as usual, but enjoy their food, just like before his absence. And this new ritual becomes gradually more natural. Also, while the father had always highlighted his work, the remaining family members now talk about their own work, which they had always wanted to do. In particular, the daughter, son, and mother begin to speak about the lives they had planned and dreamt of. In this sense, "Run Away" is not about the tragedy of a man who had shouldered the burden of a household and finally chose to disappear, but about the hope and outlook the remaining family members experience in the absence of this father and husband who had "reigned over" the family, however gently.

Kim Shin-sik, "Ek-sistence or In-sistence: Sociology of 'The Person Who Leaves Home Is No Better Than a Stranger'"
Moonji Publishing (2018)

K-픽션 023
가출

2018년 11월 9일 초판 1쇄 발행

지은이 조남주 | 옮긴이 전미세리 | 펴낸이 김재범
기획위원 전성태, 정은경, 이경재
편집 김형욱, 강민영 | 관리 강초민, 홍희표 | 디자인 나루기획
인쇄·제책 굿에그커뮤니케이션 | 종이 한솔PNS
펴낸곳 (주)아시아 | 출판등록 2006년 1월 27일 제406-2006-000004호
주소 경기도 파주시 회동길 445(서울 사무소: 서울특별시 동작구 서달로 161-1 3층)
전화 02.821.5055 | 팩스 02.821.5057 | 홈페이지 www.bookasia.org
ISBN 979-11-5662-173-7(set) | 979-11-5662-387-8(04810)
값은 뒤표지에 있습니다.

K-Fiction 023
Run Away

Written by Cho Nam-joo | Translated by Jeon Miseli
Published by ASIA Publishers | 445, Hoedong-gil, Paju-si, Gyeonggi-do, Korea
(Seoul Office:161-1, Seodal-ro, Dongjak-gu, Seoul, Korea)
Homepage Address www.bookasia.org | Tel.(822).821.5055 | Fax.(822).821.5057
First published in Korea by ASIA Publishers 2018
ISBN 979-11-5662-173-7(set) | 979-11-5662-387-8(04810)

바이링궐 에디션 한국 대표 소설

한국문학의 가장 중요하고 첨예한 문제의식을 가진 작가들의 대표작을 주제별로 선정!
하버드 한국학 연구원 및 세계 각국의 한국문학 전문 번역진이 참여한 번역 시리즈!
미국 하버드대학교와 컬럼비아대학교 동아시아학과, 캐나다 브리티시컬럼비아대학교 아시아
학과 등 해외 대학에서 교재로 채택!

바이링궐 에디션 한국 대표 소설 set 1

바이링궐 에디션 한국 대표 소설 set 2

K-포엣 시리즈는 계속됩니다.
리스트에 변동이 있을 수 있습니다.